Tor Age Bringsvaerd

When two are angry at each other

Illustrated by Tina Soli

Translated by Tonje Vetleseter

MACKENZIE SMILES
San Francisco

when **two dogs** are **angry** at each other...

When two **dragons** are **angry at** each other...

...smoke comes **out** **of** their

behinds.

Riley Lives Here

When two **witches** are angry at each other...

...they bang the door so the **whole** house **shakes.**

when two **balloons**

are angry at **each other...**

When two **angels** are angry at each other...

When two **elephants** are **angry** at each other...

...they run straight to bed and pull the covers over their ears.

When two **snowwomen** are angry at each other...

carrot noses off of each other.

...they **hide** in **separate** cookies

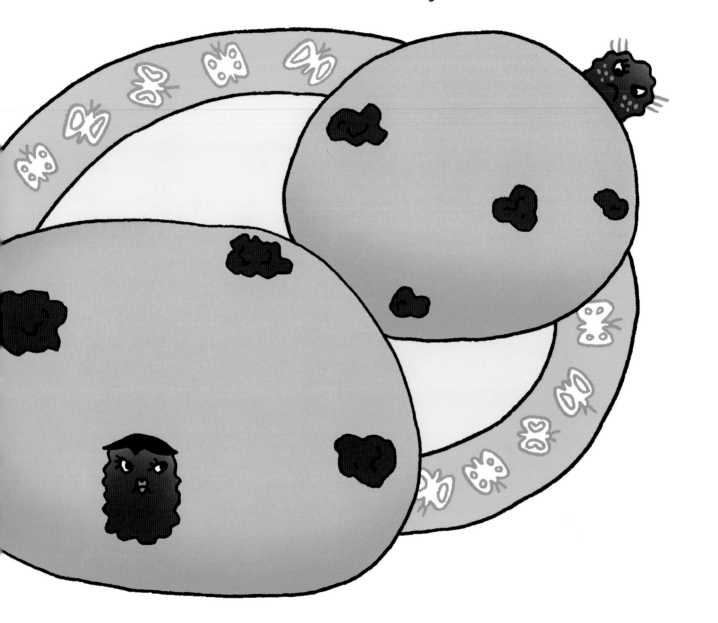

and **refuse** to **talk** to each other.

when two **lions** are **angry** at each other...

When Mommy and I are angry at each other...

But **we** don't **like to** fight.

We would **rather** give each other

a **hug**

as soon **as** possible. But...

... it is difficult to be the one to do it first. Sometimes it is Mommy. And sometimes it is me!

It is OK to disagree about something. But...

MacKenzie Smiles, LLC
San Francisco, CA

www.mackenziesmiles.com

Originally published as *Når to er Sinte på Hverandre*
Copyright © Gyldendal Norsk Forlag AS 2004 [All rights reserved]
www.gyldendal.no

Original text by Tor Age Bringsvaerd
Original illustrations by Tina Soli

Translated by Tonje Vetleseter

Art production by Bernard Prinz

ISBN 978-0-9790347-8-7

Printed in China

10 9 8 7 6 5 4 3 2 1

Distributed in the U.S. and Canada by:
Ingram Publisher Services
One Ingram Blvd.
P.O. Box 3006
LaVergne, TN 37086
(888) 800-5978

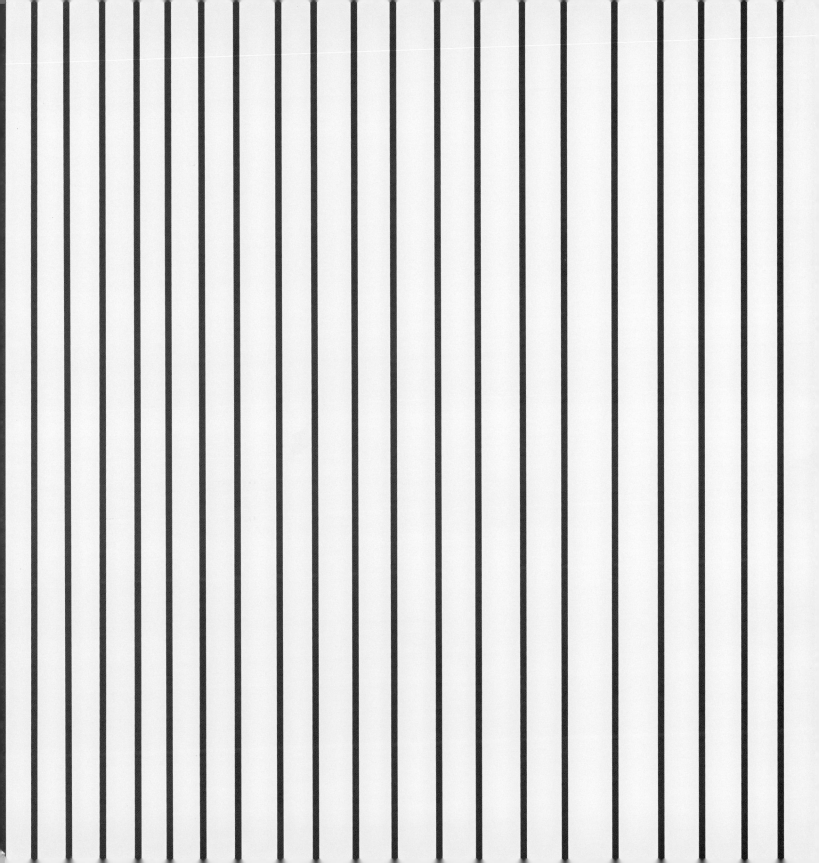